Abigail's Wish

Story by Gloria Ann Wesley

Art by Richard Rudnicki

NIMBUS
PUBLISHING

nimbus.ca

Nimbus Publishing Limited
3731 Mackintosh St, Halifax, NS B3K 5A5
(902) 455-4286 nimbus.ca

Printed and bound in Canada
NB1183
Design: Heather Bryan

Library and Archives Canada Cataloguing in Publication

Wesley, Gloria, author
Abigail's wish / story by Gloria Ann Wesley ;
art by Richard Rudnicki.

Issued in print and electronic formats.
ISBN 978-1-77108-439-0 (hardback).
—ISBN 978-1-77108-440-6 (pdf)

I. Rudnicki, Richard, illustrator II. Title.

PS8595.E6295A63 2016   jC813'.54   C2016-903709-6
                                         C2016-903710-X

Nimbus Publishing acknowledges the financial support for its publishing activities from the Government of Canada through the Canada Book Fund (CBF) and the Canada Council for the Arts, and from the Province of Nova Scotia. We are pleased to work in partnership with the Province of Nova Scotia to develop and promote our creative industries for the benefit of all Nova Scotians.

For grandchildren: Sydney, Emma, Adaya, Zaria, Byron Jr., Jace, and Malik.

Believe and follow your dreams.

Special thanks to Sherri Borden Collie and Blacie, Danielle and Blake Wright for their participation in making this book a reality.

—GW

For my family, especially my mother and father, who always encouraged me to express my creativity.

I would like to thank Blacie, Danielle and Blake, the delightful family who modelled so well for me, and Gloria Wesley for being so helpful.

—RR

Spring. Beautiful blossoms. Chirping peepers. Trees swaying in their new greenery. Pussy willows glistening in furry white coats. Rain and warmth. New births and new beginnings.

Ten-year-old Abigail Price looked in the mirror. On the wall beside it hung her Sunday dress. Beside that, an old petticoat and shift for doing chores. Today she was wearing the in-between dress, the one worn to school and for trips to Mr. Tobin's store in nearby Shelburne. All three of the dresses were old, tattered, and faded and had come from England in a barrel sent by the missionaries.

In spring, she thought, everything is new and fresh, so shouldn't she, too, have something new? All she really wanted was a brand new dress of her very own.

It was a beautiful day for the walk through Birchtown to do errands. The air was crisp and Abigail and her mother walked quickly under the overhang of long, lime-green birch branches that jutted out like an umbrella over the narrow, winding path.

Through the quiet came loud screeches of a bird flying among the trees.

Abigail was startled. Her heart pounded as she
stopped cold in her tracks.

"Don't be afraid, Abigail," her mother said calmly.
"We are safe. Where's your smile? This promises to
be a special day."

Abigail nodded, knowing she had to get used to
her new home and all its strange creatures.

Abigail let the word "safe" slide off her tongue.
The American Revolution, with all its noise, bad
dreams, and fear, was over. She and her mother
and father had been transported to Shelburne,
Nova Scotia, with nearly three thousand others.

With thirty sails like huge white birds, the ships had taken them from New York in 1783. Nine days on the Atlantic Ocean. How the ship had tossed and rolled on the dark and endless sea. The fluffy white clouds and sunshine soon disappeared and the rain grew fierce and the wind roared. A strange sickness in her belly lasted for days and with only water, bread, and cheese to eat each day, her stomach growled like a bear.

And now, a few years later, everyone was calling this colony named Birchtown, home.

Yes, it's a special day, Abigail thought. Each year the entire colony waited for the big moment: the birth of the first spring babies in Birchtown.

Her aunt, Dinah Johnson, was expecting a baby any day now and Abigail was excited. They would be visiting her that afternoon. But she was waiting on her wish to be fulfilled for a new dress.

"Maybe in the spring," her mother had said.

Times are hard, her father had said. "People are starving and there's little work. Be thankful, Abigail, that for now, I've found work and we have a little food and some place to sleep. And new things, well…."

She knew the rest. Her wish was just a dream.

Abigail looked around her aunt's hut. The news that Dinah would be having a baby had spread quickly. In the tiny room, a midwife sat next to a fire pit. Aunt Dinah sat on a small cot in the corner, her belly surging like a mountain beneath a patchwork quilt reaching for the sky. Abigail saw no sign of a baby.

"Have you picked out any names yet?" Abigail asked.

"Isaac, if it's a boy, and Harriet, if it's a girl," Dinah replied.

With a quivering hand, Abigail's mother patted the quilted mound. After stroking Dinah's hair and cradling her in her arms, she announced it was time to leave. "We'll stop in on the way back from Mr. Tobin's store," she said. "Maybe, with a little luck, we will have this baby."

The birth would mean a big celebration: people would bring what they could spare to eat, and the singing and laughter and dancing would be such fun. Surely, a new dress was needed for such a celebration, Abigail hoped.

Days earlier, Abigail and her mother had travelled to Shelburne to clean Mrs. Spinney's house. For pay, they were able to take vegetables from the bin in the cellar. They had sorted the vegetables into two piles: one pile to keep, and one pile to trade for goods at Mr. Tobin's store.

Today Abigail walked briskly behind her mother, swinging her basket of vegetables. Maybe her mother would trade them for some fabric to make her dress. At least that's what she was hoping.

Abigail loved the odd smell that tickled her nose
when she opened the door at Mr. Tobin's store.

Barrels of cornmeal, beans, molasses, salted beef
and pork, and brown sugar stood along the walls.
A huge scale hung above the counter. There were
all kinds of tools: augers, chisels, spades, saws,
shovels, hammers, and planes waiting to be bought
by the settlers.

"Help yourself to a treat," Mr. Tobin said, smiling at her.
"Just take one."

Abigail's taste buds were suddenly delighted as she chewed a piece of black licorice.

Abigail wandered about the store. There were
so many wonderful things. Stopping beside the
summer fabric, she stared at the bolts of flowered
and plain cotton, piles of silk, satin, and chintz.
She fancied herself in pretty petticoats, gowns,
caps, and aprons.

If only her mother would exchange the vegetables
for a few yards.

She watched as Mr. Tobin put the salt meat and a small jug of molasses into her mother's bag.

"Here you go, Abigail," her mother said. "You can carry the cornmeal and beans in your basket."

Abigail took the basket and looked inside. There was no fabric for a new dress.

Back at Aunt Dinah's there was quite a commotion.

Outside, people milled about. Inside, Dinah was
holding a small bundle wrapped in the quilt she'd
worn before. A round brown face with a full head
of black curls peeped out.

"A boy," Dinah said as Abigail and her mother stared in delight.

A big grin brightened Abigail's face. She watched as people came and went, bringing little gifts of food or something they had made for baby Isaac.

Abigail, too, would make something for the baby. She would use the leftover scraps of the quilts her mother made.

Thinking about that, Abigail's hopes for a new dress returned. Maybe they could stop at the church and see if anyone from Shelburne had donated clothes from their spring cleaning. Maybe she would even find a child's dress that fit; they were always scarce, but her mother was skilful at making old clothes into something new.

"Can we stop by the church and see if there are any donations?" Abigail asked. Her mother smiled. They both enjoyed searching through the barrels to see if there was anything useful.

Abigail explained to Reverend George how she was hoping to find a new dress to properly celebrate the birth of Dinah's baby boy. But again, she was disappointed.

"A cold spring has kept everyone from their spring cleaning," he told them, "but I expect the donations will arrive soon."

Mrs. George looked at Abigail with a sad face.

Abigail's heart sank.

At home, Abigail gathered up the leftover pieces of her mother's quilts to make a tiny one for her new baby cousin.

There was not enough cloth left to make anything for herself. She would just have to forget having a new dress and wait on donations.

Nearly two weeks later, while Abigail was busy peeling potatoes, Reverend George stopped by to pay a visit. His face was glowing like a candle.

"Come, Abigail," he said, "I have something for you." He handed her a parcel tied in brown twine. "Mrs. George wanted you have this."

What could it be?

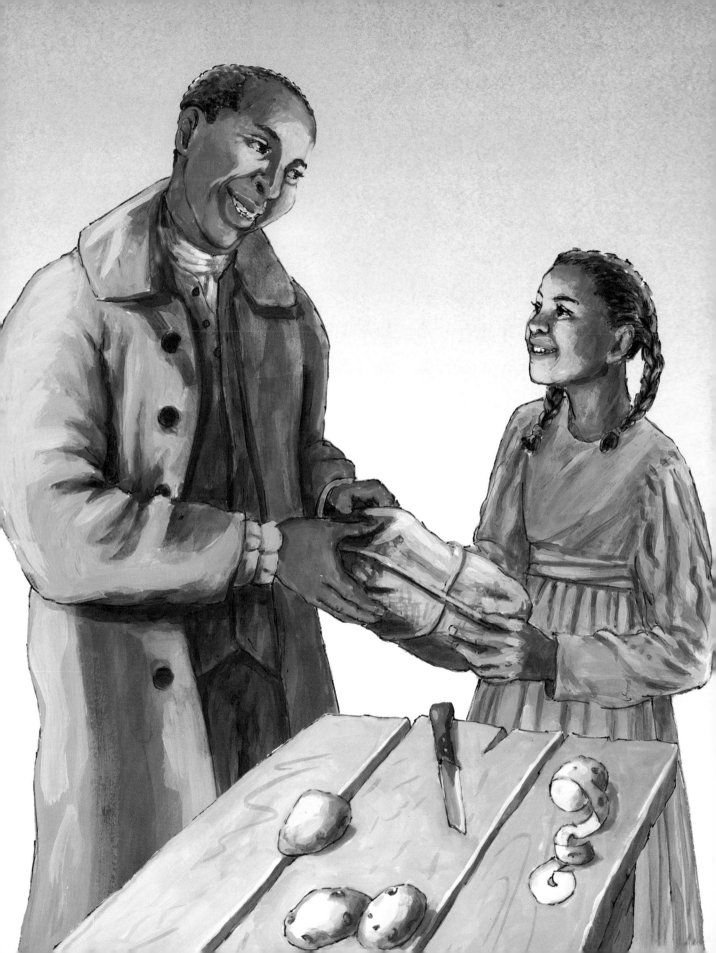

That Sunday morning, Abigail was up just as the sun glided above the horizon. It was going to be a day for celebrating the miracles of spring at church.

At breakfast, she gobbled down some bread and weak tea. Then she was off to get dressed behind the long curtain that separated her bedroom from the kitchen.

In the mirror, Abigail gazed proudly for a long time. Then, pinning a bouquet of buttercups to her new green dress, and with her long braids flapping like wings, she twirled about and whispered, "Thank you, Mrs. George, for making my wish come true."